SCARY TALES RETOLD™

SNOW WHITE AND THE SEVEN TROLLS

by Wiley Blevins • illustrated by Steve Cox

RED CHAIR
•PRESS•

Please visit our website at **www.redchairpress.com** for more high-quality products for young readers.

About the Author

Wiley Blevins has taught elementary school in both the United States and South America. He has also written over 70 books for children and 15 for teachers, as well as created reading programs for schools in the U.S. and Asia with Scholastic, Macmillan/McGraw-Hill, Houghton-Mifflin Harcourt, and other publishers. Wiley currently lives and writes in New York City.

About the Artist

Steve Cox lives in London, England. He first designed toys and packaging for other people's characters. But he decided to create his own characters and turned full time to illustrating. When he is not drawing books he plays lead guitar in a rock band.

Publisher's Cataloging-In-Publication Data

Blevins, Wiley.
   Snow White and the seven trolls / by Wiley Blevins ; illustrated by Steve Cox.

   pages : illustrations ; cm. -- (Scary tales retold)

   Summary: "As in the classic tale, our Snow White falls under the spell of the evil Queen when she bites into a golden apple. Are the seven trolls coming to save her or to trick the princes who come to break the spell? Only one troll decides his future lies with Snow White, not his fellow trolls and their newly stolen riches"--Provided by publisher.
   Issued also as an ebook.
   ISBN: 978-1-63440-105-0 (library hardcover)
   ISBN: 978-1-63440-106-7 (paperback)

   11. Princesses--Juvenile fiction. 2. Trolls--Juvenile fiction. 3. Charms--Juvenile fiction. 4. Princesses--Fiction. 5. Trolls--Fiction. 6. Charms--Fiction. 7. Fairy tales. 8. Horror tales. I. Cox, Steve, 1961- II. Title. III. Title: Based on (work) Snow White and the seven dwarfs.

PZ7.B618652 Sn 2016
[E]   2015906803

Scary Tales Retold first published by:
Red Chair Press LLC   PO Box 333   South Egremont, MA 01258-0333

Printed in the United States of America
Distributed in the U.S. by Lerner Publisher Services. www.lernerbooks.com

0516 1 CBGF16

In a dark, faraway forest lived a queen.
She was the most beautiful queen in the land.

But when she looked into her mirror, it didn't show her perfect face or shiny crown. It showed how she looked on the inside.

Wicked.

"Mirror, mirror on the wall," said the queen. "Who is the most beautiful of them all?"

A ghostly face appeared in the mirror. "It is Snow White," laughed the face.

The queen went into a rage.
"Who is this Snow White?" she screamed.

The mirror showed a beautiful girl playing
in the forest. Her hair was as black as night.
Her skin was as white as snow.

The wicked queen began to keep an eye on
Snow White. She hid behind trees and watched
her pick flowers in the forest. She sent the birds
to follow her as Snow White fetched water at
the river.

With each year, Snow White grew more and more beautiful. So on her eighteenth birthday, the queen sent Snow White a present. It was a red and juicy apple wrapped in gold paper. But the queen had put a terrible curse on it.

When Snow White bit into the apple, she fell into a deep sleep. The queen screeched with joy. "She will sleep forever unless kissed by a worthy prince. Only that kiss will break the curse."

Nearby, seven mean and ugly trolls heard the
queen's screeches. Their names were Smelly,
Stinky, Icky, Yucky, Slimy, Gooey, and Pickles.
They ran to find the sleeping Snow White.

But they weren't there to rescue Snow White. You see, trolls are oh so sneaky. The trolls took Snow White to their little cave in the forest. They placed her on a bed of grass.

Then the trolls sent word throughout the land that they needed a prince to break the curse. If the prince brought Snow White the perfect gift, she would become his queen— the most beautiful queen in all the land.

But Smelly, Stinky, Icky, Yucky, Slimy, and Gooey had no plan to tell a prince how to break the curse. Their plan was to take the riches each prince would bring and keep it all for themselves. You see, trolls are also very greedy.

But Pickles was not like the other trolls.
He was smaller and made to do all the
work—especially the cooking. He cooked all
day and night. And when he wasn't cooking,
he was cleaning and shining his pots and pans.
Pickles felt sad for Snow White.

Each night Pickles would place a single red
rose in Snow White's hand. He would look
at the moon and wish that one day a worthy
prince would arrive.

One by one, prince after prince came to see
Snow White. They marveled at her beauty.
Each brought a present better than the
prince before.

The riches piled higher and higher. The trolls laughed and snorted with glee each time a prince left with no luck breaking the curse.

Finally one day a prince from the poorest country in the land showed up.

"I have nothing to give Snow White but my love," he said.

Pickles knew this prince was "the one."

But Smelly, Stinky, Icky, Yucky, Slimy, and Gooey screamed at the prince to leave. "Without gold or silver or other riches you will not be able to break the curse."

The poor prince hung his head as he shuffled back to his horse to return home.

Pickles snuck up behind him and whispered, "Please dear sir, give Snow White a kiss goodbye."

The prince leaned down and gave Snow White a soft kiss. "Oh dear," she sighed as she woke up and saw his old, worn clothes. "I so hoped I would get kissed by a rich prince. But I will be your queen if I can take Pickles with us."

The prince agreed. Pickles quickly gathered his pots and pans. And even though the prince had no riches, the three lived happily ever after.

Of course, that's because Pickles had hidden all the gold and silver inside his pots and pans. Smelly, Stinky, Icky, Yucky, Slimy, and Gooey were left with nothing and no one to cook their meals.

THE END